T0193007

All the water

a richard jackson book

atheneum books for young readers

new york london toronto sydney

in the world

by George Ella Lyon
and Katherine Tillotson

...is all the water

in the world.

Water

flows from the hose.

It wobbles

in blue pools.

It

fills

your

cup

up.

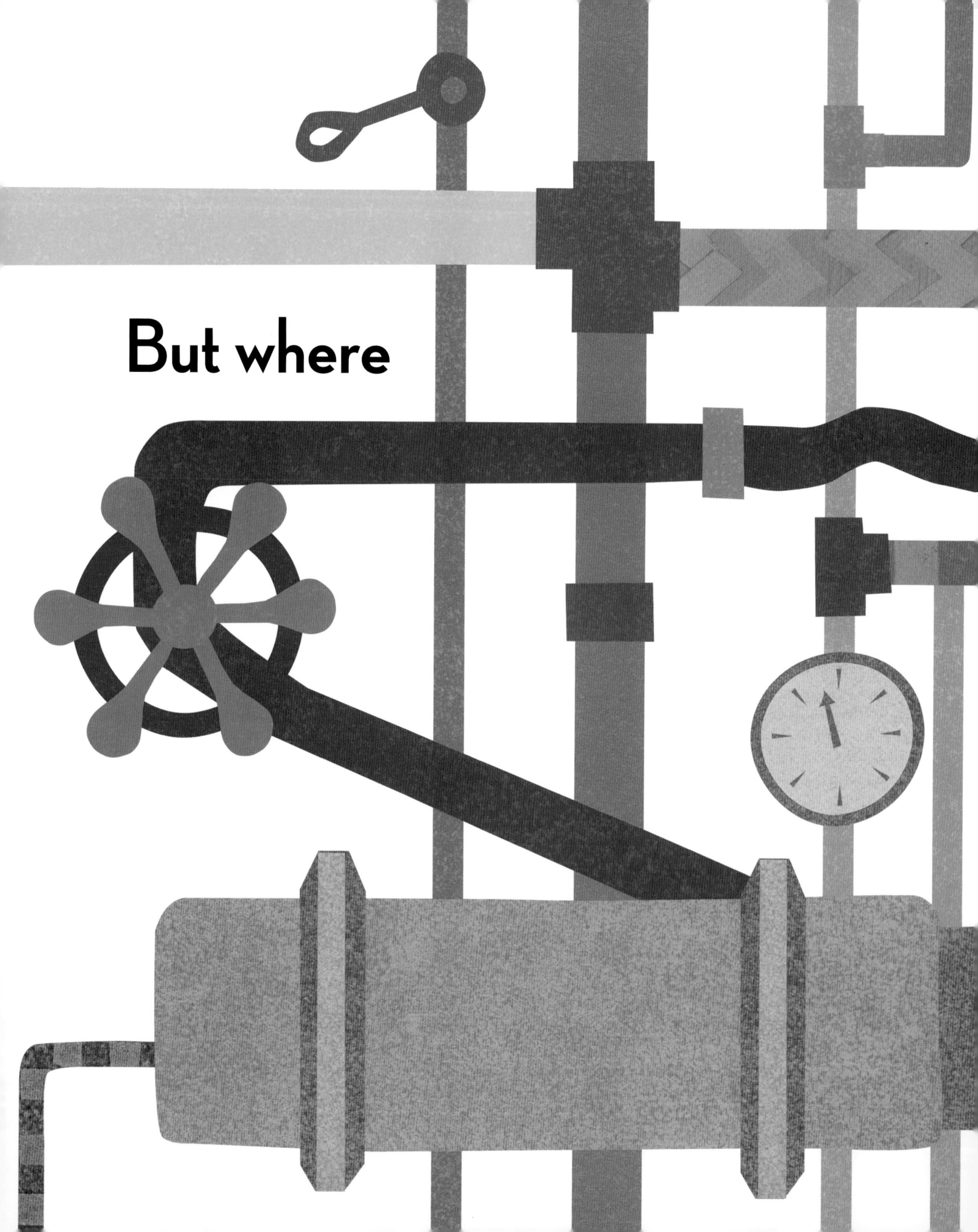
But where

does it come
from?

Water doesn't come.
It goes.
Around.

That rain

that cascaded from clouds

and meandered down mountains,

that wavered over waterfalls

then slipped into rivers

and opened into oceans,

that rain has been here before.

Thirsty air

licks it from lakes

sips it from ponds

guzzles it from oceans

swirl up
and this wet air

till it's crowded into clouds
where it hangs hotly around
till cool air bumps through
and honey, those clouds
just
let
it
go
and
rain
rain

rain!

Tap dance
avalanche
stampede
of drips and drops and drumming—

a wealth of water.

But far away

it's a different day—

no sound but wind

empty cup again

dry grasses rustle

dirt's just dust.

Everything waits

for an open gate

in a wall of clouds

for rain sweet and loud

to fill the well

and start the stream.

Honey,
living things dream
of water

for all to drink
use in tub or sink
wash in, splash in.

This wet wonder
means grow
means life will flow

through tigers
through trees.

Through you

and through me.

All
all
All together

all
all
now

all so precious—do not waste it.
And delicious—we can taste it.

Keep it clear, keep it clean . . .

keep Earth

For Pete Seeger, Wendell Berry, Gurney Norman,
and all who work to save the water of life

And for Bernie Stoddard, who is just learning to swim in it
—G. E. L.

For Dick Jackson, dowser, editor, friend
—K. T.

For more information on the water cycle,
visit the *All the Water in the World* book page on
TEACH.SimonandSchuster.net or KIDS.SimonandSchuster.com!

ATHENEUM BOOKS
FOR YOUNG READERS
An imprint of Simon & Schuster
Children's Publishing Division
1230 Avenue of the Americas,
New York, New York 10020
Text copyright © 2011 by George Ella Lyon
Illustrations copyright © 2011 by Katherine Tillotson
All rights reserved, including the right of reproduction
in whole or in part in any form.
ATHENEUM BOOKS FOR YOUNG READERS is a registered trademark of
Simon & Schuster, Inc. For information about special discounts for bulk
purchases, please contact Simon & Schuster Special Sales
at 1-866-506-1949 or business@simonandschuster.com.
The Simon & Schuster Speakers Bureau can bring authors to your live event.
For more information or to book an event, contact the Simon & Schuster
Speakers Bureau at 1-866-248-3049 or visit our website at
www.simonspeakers.com.
Book design by Ann Bobco
The text for this book is set in Neutraface.
The illustrations for this book are rendered digitally.
Manufactured in China • 0622 SCP
13 14 15 16 17 18 19 20
Library of Congress Cataloging-in-Publication Data
Lyon, George Ella, 1949–
All the water in the world / George Ella Lyon ;
illustrated by KatherineTillotson. — 1st ed. p. cm.
"A Richard Jackson book."
ISBN 978-1-4169-7130-6
ISBN 978-1-4424-3295-6 (eBook)
1. Hydrologic cycle—Juvenile literature.
I. Tillotson, Katherine, ill. II. Title.
GB848.L96 2011
551.48—dc22
2010029530